D0100087

CALGARY PUBLIC LIBRARY

JUL — 2009

THE GREAT DOG WASH

Because one sang "Dog Wash, Dog Wash"
while the other was patiently being lathered and rinsed,
I lovingly dedicate this book to Elizabeth and Fluffy.
—S. B.

For my girls, Ruth, Jo, and Iz.
—R. N.

ACKNOWLEDGMENTS

My thanks go to my parents, Betsy, my family, and Jane and Greg for
the many kinds of support you have given me, as well as Joyce, Shelly, and David
for giving me this chance. I would also like to thank Holly, Beth, Tiffany, Ginger,
and everyone on the Midsouth SCBWI board for being the best darn cyber writing group possible.
But most of all, I would like to thank the young people in my life: Gaines, Will, Clarke,
Elliot, Ty, Hallie, Adam, McKenna, Elizabeth, Simon, and Henry for listening to all my stories.
—S. B.

Special thanks to my models, Alta, Roxy, and Jojo.
—R. N.

SIMON & SCHUSTER BOOKS FOR YOUNG READERS
An imprint of Simon & Schuster Children's Publishing Division
1230 Avenue of the Americas, New York, New York 10020
Text copyright © 2009 by Michelle Braeuner
Illustrations copyright © 2009 by Robert Neubecker
All rights reserved, including the right of reproduction in whole or in part in any form.
SIMON & SCHUSTER BOOKS FOR YOUNG READERS is a trademark of Simon & Schuster, Inc.
Book design by Laurent Linn
The text for this book is set in Soup Bone.
The illustrations for this book are rendered digitally.
Manufactured in China
2 4 6 8 10 9 7 5 3 1
Library of Congress Cataloging-in-Publication Data
Braeuner, Shellie.
The great dog wash / by Shellie Braeuner ; illustrated by Robert Neubecker.
p. cm.
Summary: Rhyming text welcomes the reader to a dog wash that goes awry when someone brings their cat.
ISBN: 978-1-4169-7116-0 (hardcover : alk. paper)
[1. Stories in rhyme. 2. Dogs—Fiction. 3. Cats—Fiction. 4. Humorous stories.] I. Neubecker, Robert, ill. II. Title.
PZ8.3.B7322Gre 2009 [E]—dc22 2008006705

first
edition

THE GREAT DOG WASH

By Shellie Braeuner

Illustrated by Robert Neubecker

Simon & Schuster Books for Young Readers

NEW YORK　　LONDON　　TORONTO　　SYDNEY

Big dogs and small dogs,
come one and all dogs.
We're having a **dog wash** today!

Slippery, slobbery,
do a good jobbery.
Wash all that dog smell away.

Tall dogs

or **round** dogs,

store dogs

or found dogs.

Short hair and long hair, some with quite strong hair.

You'll each get your
turn in the tub.

Oh, gee! Look at that!
Now, who brought a **cat**?

Watch out!

Be careful!

Oh, no!

Just what we need,
a doggy stampede.

And up the street
all of them go.

Where could they be?
In the yard with the tree.
Now, how will we ever—

Bring sprinklers and hoses.
We'll clean all those noses!
And somebody please close the gate.

We'll fix all their troubles,
with soap and with bubbles,
while dogs are all watching the tree.

And somebody oughta
turn on all that water . . .

for the Great Dog Wash

jamboree!

Big dogs and small dogs
now clean and brushed dogs.
They each have their own sense of **style**.

It was fun but hard work
when those dogs went **berserk**,

so it's good that we're done . . . .

for a while.